MAKE IT NOW!

MONSTERS

11 Paper Finger Puppets
to Punch Out, Cut, Fold, and Glue, with 10 Scenes to Color—
Plus Stickers!

Marcel Pixel

Houghton Mifflin Harcourt
Boston New York

D1489369

Follow the instructions to create your own monsters, and get ready for adventure!

Trouble is brewing in the monster world. Color the monsters and ghoulish scenes, then make the monsters come to life!

Watch out, Demon!

You'll never catch me, Robomonster!

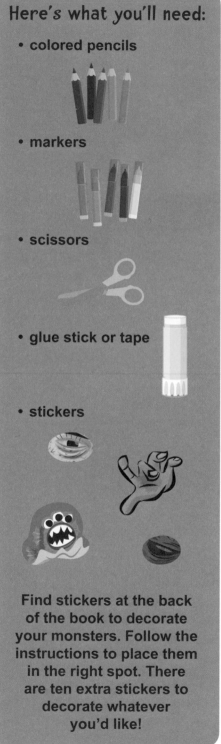

Here's what you'll need:

- colored pencils
- markers
- scissors
- glue stick or tape
- stickers

Find stickers at the back of the book to decorate your monsters. Follow the instructions to place them in the right spot. There are ten extra stickers to decorate whatever you'd like!

The Finger Puppets

Monsters Ready to Punch Out

At the back of the book, there are four monsters that are ready for you to punch out. Carefully detach the pieces for each monster by gently pressing along the perforated lines. Then follow the illustrated directions on the next page.

Monsters to Cut Out and Color

There are seven monsters to color, decorate, cut out, and construct on your own throughout the book. Find them by looking for this symbol (which comes in different colors) at the top of each page. (The symbol appears on any page you should pull out.)

To start creating these monsters, put this book on a flat surface, then gently pull out the four pages labeled with the same color symbols.

1 Finish coloring in each of the monsters.

2 Attach the stickers using the dotted lines as a guide for proper placement.

3 Following the outline of each monster, carefully cut along the solid lines—not the dotted lines. The dotted lines are for folding. To cut out the holes (marked by a circle with an X inside), gently fold the paper, make a small cut along the hole's solid outline, unfold, and then carefully continue to cut along the solid line until the hole is gone.

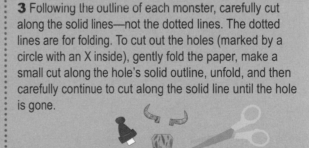

How to make your finger puppets

1 Fold each puppet by bending the paper tabs and folding the monster's mouth shut along the dotted lines.

2 Glue or tape each tab in numerical order, as indicated by the numbers. For example, number 1 on the front of the puppet gets glued to number one on the back side of the puppet. Start with the top of the head, then connect the bottom, then seal the back of the puppet.

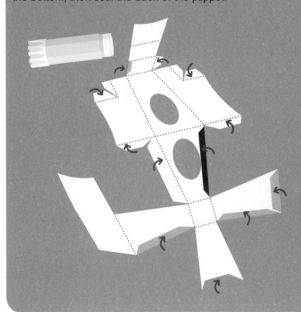

3 Add the arms, horns, and accessories, either sliding them into the pre-cut slits or gluing or taping them into the corresponding areas of the puppet marked with a dotted line.

Yeti

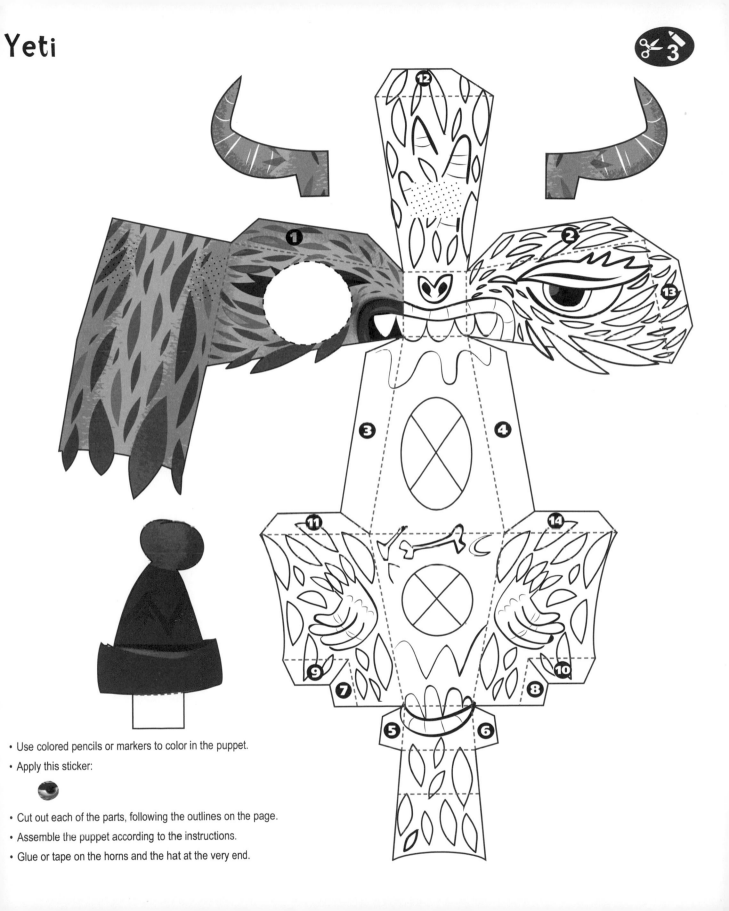

- Use colored pencils or markers to color in the puppet.
- Apply this sticker:
- Cut out each of the parts, following the outlines on the page.
- Assemble the puppet according to the instructions.
- Glue or tape on the horns and the hat at the very end.

Ghost

- Use colored pencils or markers to color in the puppet.
- Apply these stickers:

- Cut out each of the parts, following the outlines on the page.
- Assemble the puppet according to the instructions.
- Glue or tape on the hat at the very end.

2 **1**

12

13

4 **3**

14

11

6 **5**

8 **7**

10 **9**

Werewolf

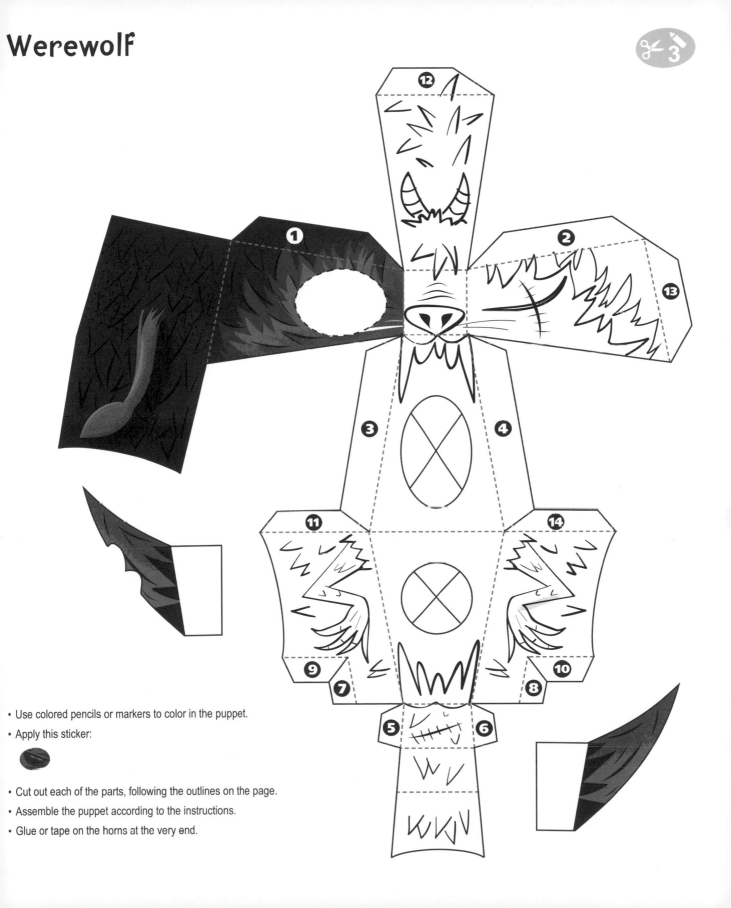

- Use colored pencils or markers to color in the puppet.
- Apply this sticker:

- Cut out each of the parts, following the outlines on the page.
- Assemble the puppet according to the instructions.
- Glue or tape on the horns at the very end.

② ① ⑫ ⑬ ④ ③ ⑭ ⑪ ⑥ ⑤ ⑧ ⑦ ⑩ ⑨

Vampire

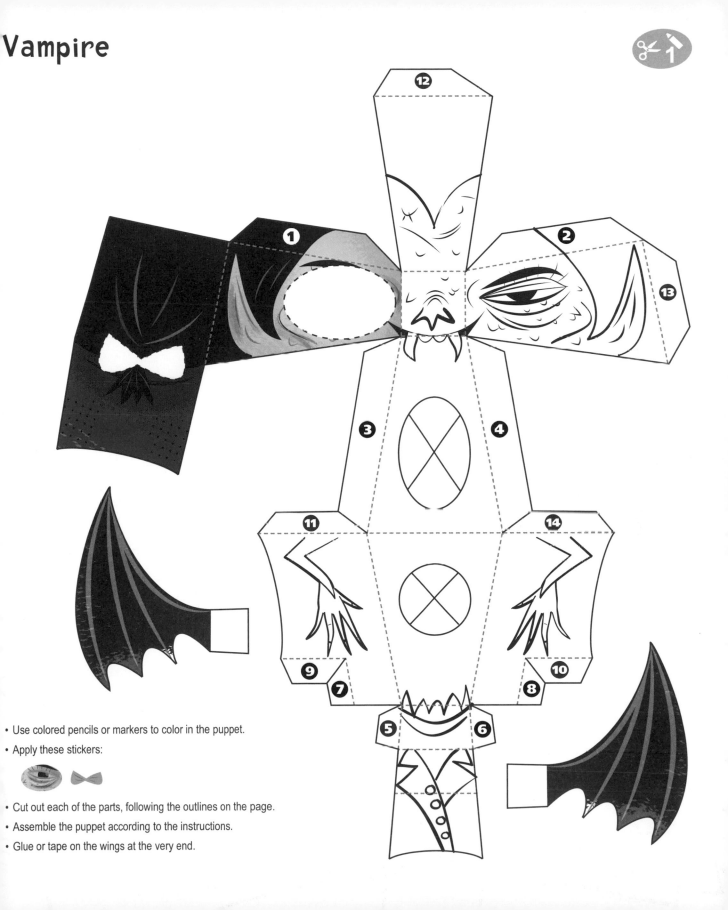

- Use colored pencils or markers to color in the puppet.
- Apply these stickers:

- Cut out each of the parts, following the outlines on the page.
- Assemble the puppet according to the instructions.
- Glue or tape on the wings at the very end.

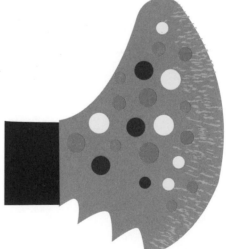
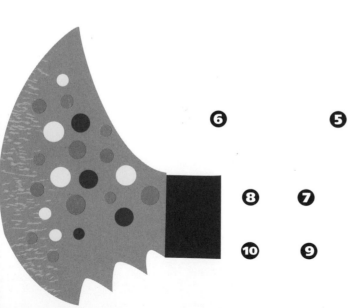

Mummy

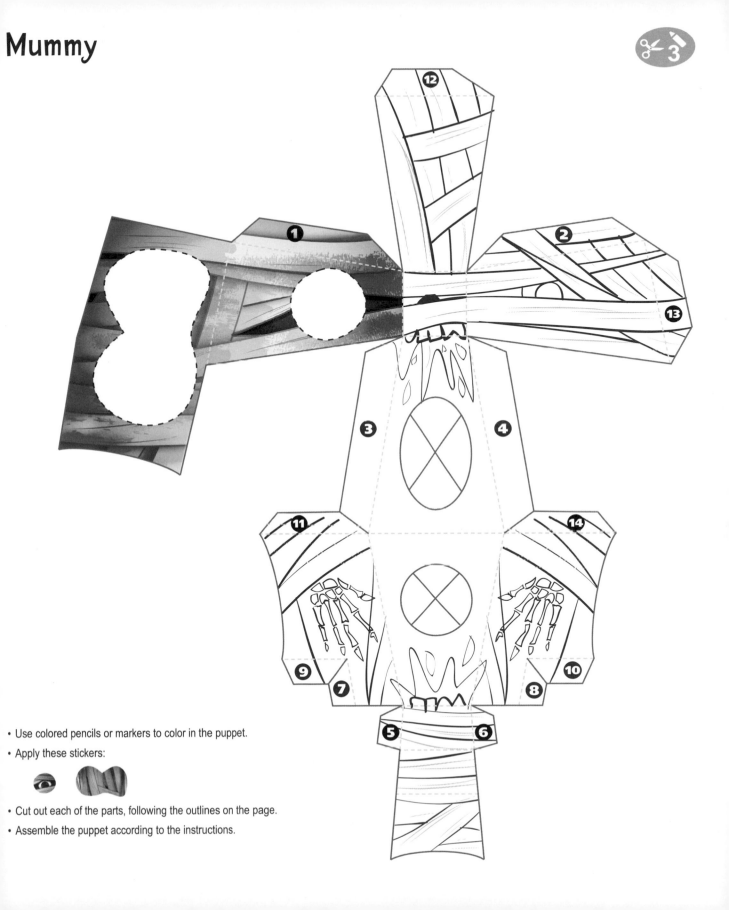

- Use colored pencils or markers to color in the puppet.
- Apply these stickers:
- Cut out each of the parts, following the outlines on the page.
- Assemble the puppet according to the instructions.

2 1

12

13

4 3

14

11

6 5

8 7

10 9

Zombie

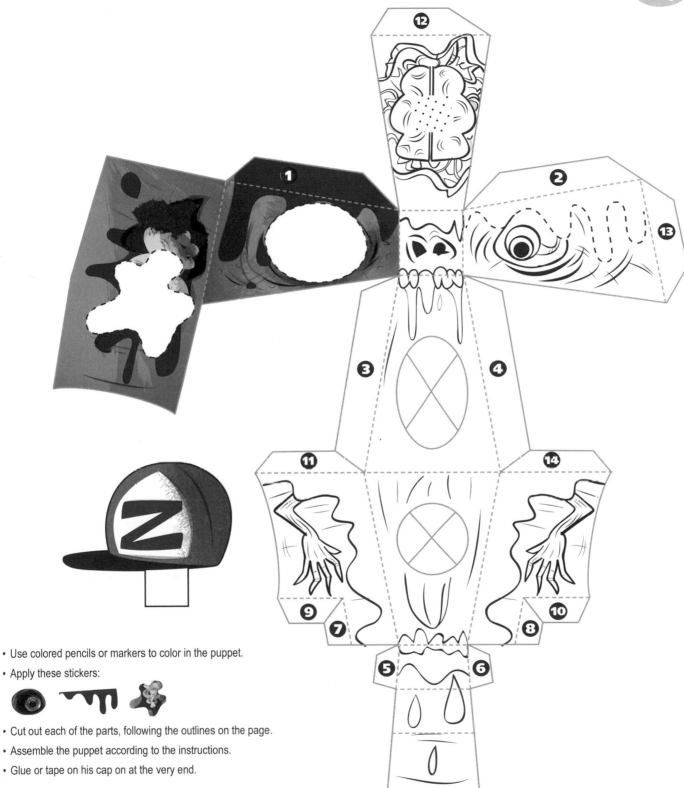

- Use colored pencils or markers to color in the puppet.
- Apply these stickers:
- Cut out each of the parts, following the outlines on the page.
- Assemble the puppet according to the instructions.
- Glue or tape on his cap on at the very end.

2 **1**

12

13

4

3

14

11

6 **5**

8 **7**

10 **9**

Alien

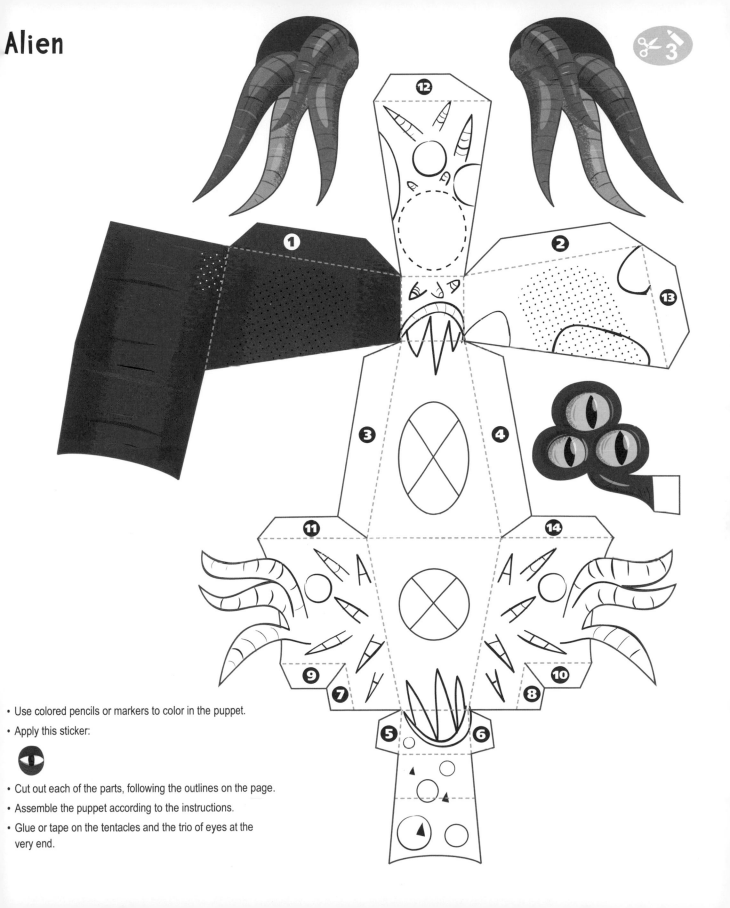

- Use colored pencils or markers to color in the puppet.
- Apply this sticker:
- Cut out each of the parts, following the outlines on the page.
- Assemble the puppet according to the instructions.
- Glue or tape on the tentacles and the trio of eyes at the very end.